Betting it All
in Deadwood

Karaoke, Cards, & Clutter Series
A Chic Lit story about Maribeth Thorp
A tale of friendship, love, trust, romance, and life in general

Book #1

Lynn Donovan

Note: A version of this story, Karaoke, Cards, & Clutter, was previously published in the Lost and Found in Deadwood anthology 2023. The author has made significant changes, reduced, and expanded the story in this novel for the series.

Copyright

This book is a work of fiction. The names, characters, places, and incidents are all products of the author's imagination and are not to be construed as real. Any resemblances to persons, organizations, events, or locales are entirely coincidental.

The book contains material protected under International and Federal Copyright Laws and Treaties. All rights are reserved with the exceptions of quotes used in reviews. No part of this book may be reproduced or transmitted in any form or by any means, electronic or mechanical, including photocopying, recording, or by any information storage system without express written permission from the author.

This book was written by a human and not Artificial Intelligence (A.I.).

This book cannot be used to train Artificial Intelligence (A.I.).

About this Series

Karaoke, Cards, & Clutter Series

Maribeth Thorp is looking for a new start in Deadwood, South Dakota. Having left the boyfriend of eight years, she is desperate for a new beginning. Gambling on a house deed she won after a successful night of cards, she moves into the home on a blind bet. As things unfold, Maribeth finds herself in one dilemma after another. Can she resolve life's unexpected surprises and maintain her sanity at the same time? Or will it all come crashing down on top of her in one giant epic failure?

Introduction

Betting it All in Deadwood Professional Organizer, Maribeth Thorp has a secret. With her photographic memory and her father's aptitude for winning, she never loses… at cards anyway. At thirty-one she gives herself a major declutter by leaving her dead-end relationship of eight years. Now, all bets are off. She is broke, desperate, and homeless. Until she finds a house deed she won a while back. Now, she is betting it all in Deadwood. Will this blind bet pay off?

Acknowledgements

Thank you to everybody in my life who has contributed in one way or another to the writing of this book. My husband, my children, my children-in-law, and my grandchildren. You all are my unconditional fans. My BETA reader and grammar guru who make me look gooder than I am. [Bad grammar intended.] My fellow author friends who chat with me daily to exchange ideas, encourage, maintain sanity, and keep me from being a total recluse/hermit.

Mostly I thank God for the talent he has given me. I hope to hear you say, "Well done, my good and faithful servant," when I cross the Jordan and run into your arms—Many, many years from now. :)..

LYNN DONOVAN

Chapter One

"You are two-hundred feet from your destination."
Siri announces from my cell phone. But all I see is
extremely weedy and rough, extremely angled,
extremely overgrown land that goes straight up, up,
up. My eyes drop to the street. Is that a driveway? I
can see a detached garage at street level with a short
crushed granite rock-covered driveway. I pick up
the deed laying in my passenger seat and double-
check the address.

"Seriously?" I say to no one.

My name is Maribeth Thorp. You might be
wondering what I'm doing looking for a house when

all I have is a deed and an address. Well, it happened like this…

You see, I have a gambling problem. The problem is— I'm good at it. Really good at it. Any game that involves counting and recall, I can win with great efficiency. Poker is my game and, although I'm from Colorado originally, any form of poker is my *pièce de résistance*. Five card stud, Texas Hold 'em, Five Card Draw, or Seven Card Draw… I can play them all.

One thing my dad passed on to me was his genetics for mathematics and a photographic memory. I know what cards have been played and can calculate the next probabilities in my head, like he did, and win games, like he did—

… until he didn't.

Thank goodness I had these skills or else Momma and I would have been living on the streets after Daddy committed suicide.

So, here I am, fifteen years after my Daddy's unintentional lesson that you don't always win, moving to Deadwood, South Dakota. I have just this minute found the house that I won a while back in a poker game. I've never been here in my life so all I have to go by is an address on a deed. Someone didn't learn the lesson I had learned about collateral and houses. Or they were too desperate to heed the wisdom. Their loss was my ga— well looking at that drive, I'm not sure what to call it: gain, money pit; could go either way.

Behind the garage, there is an incredibly long, multi-level set of red-wood stairs that goes up to something, surely it's a house. I can't tell from where I sit in my car. The overgrowth is strangling my view.

"Are you kidding me?" I scream. "Is there no other way to get to that house?"

Is this even the right place? I stare at my phone screen.

Siri says cheerfully, "You have arrived."

"Arrived where!?" I yell at the lady in my phone.

Just to be sure, I google the legal description, which I remember without looking back at the deed, and it shows the exact same location. I crane my neck to look through the windshield at the steep grade of green bushes, grass, and weeds.

"Oh wait, there *is* a house up there." I utter aloud. "Great, now I'm talking to myself!"

I sigh and pull into the short driveway that ends at a closed garage door. It looks a lot like a carriage house door. Painted white with black wrought iron decor depicting fake hinges and pull handles, it's not fooling me. There are no horses inside. I know it's just an overhead garage door, but it does look really nice. So does the house, now that I can get a better look.

It's just… those sinister stairs.

"Ugh!" I bury my face in my hands against the steering wheel. This is what my life has come to? At thirty-one, my savings is depleted, I'm all-in in a town I've never been to before, in a house that is a blind bet on the inside. I don't know if it's furnished, or whatever, all because I can't pick a good man as well as I can play cards.

Kiley, my car, is really running rough. I'm not sure if it's the altitude, the alternator, spark plugs, or not-so-great gas that I filled her with, even though I paid for the medium-priced grade. She is struggling and I'm praying she will keep going. This may be all she's got left in her. "Just get me to the driveway, ol' girl," I beg my car.

Black smoke is billowing from her tailpipe. "Come on, girl."

Siri is non-emotional when she announces, "You have reached your final destination."

I am where I'm supposed to be, bringing me back to my task at hand. I crane my neck, again, to look beyond my rearview mirror, through the darkened sun-protective tinting on the windshield, to see the house.

It was lovely. Sort of a dark harvest gold painted clapboard home with dark brown trim. I look around at the overgrown lot.

"Is the long, wooden stairway the only way to get to the house?" I ask nobody one more time just in case I'm wrong. Really hoping I am wrong.

Having eased Kiley into the driveway, I didn't have to kill the engine. It died on its own. Poor Kiley. Putting her in park, I turn the key to off and cup it in my fist.

This is the place.

This is my house.

Tears burst from my eyes, like an emoji with streams pouring down its face. "This is my house," I sob.

I stare at the closed garage door, wondering how I'm going to get inside. The quit-claim deed making it mine was all I had— no key, no remote, nothing. I look at the deed as if it will show me how to gain access.

"Oh!" I exclaim. Written at the top right corner were four numbers. 1876. A code? Was it the code for the garage door? I walk to a small box at eye level on the garage door frame and punch in the numbers, then push "enter." The garage door groans and squeaks like it is in need of some WD-40, but it begins to rise.

I sighed with relief. At least I can get inside the garage. I walk toward a door at the back where a metal box is hung. Guessing, hoping, I open the box and find a garage door opener to clip on my visor and two keys. They had to be to the door of the house. I lift all three and head toward that long set of stairs. Bushes and vine weeds tangled in the grass threaten to trip me as I climb. I wonder if there's an affordable lawn service available around here? Or a kid with a lawnmower?

My need for oxygen increases with each step. Huffing and puffing I slowly get closer to the front door. I am not used to this altitude, I say to myself, but that's ridiculous because it's nearly a thousand feet lower than Denver. I will not admit my trouble breathing has anything to do with my ability to climb stairs. Since my break-up, I haven't been to the gym, or walked around a block. Let's face it, I'm completely out of shape.

Pausing on one of the last landings where the stairs turn ninety degrees and keep going, I turn to look out across the incline. What a lovely view! Hopefully I won't pass out before I can get inside, but if I do, at least the last thing my eyes take in is this gorgeous panorama.

I insert one key in the doorknob, it turns over. I insert the other in the dead bolt, it turns. I push the door open and walk in.

"Wow. This is nice." I breathe the words, because I'm still trying to catch my breath.

"Here I go, talking to myself, again." I shake my head. But it really was a nice house. Not cluttered at all. It looked like a model home with modern furnishings, and just right, impersonal wall hangings. Spotless. Not a speck of dirt or dust anywhere. Was there a cleaning service taking care of the place that I was not aware of? I shrug and turn to go back down to retrieve my things.

But slam to a halt because of the large, muscular body blocking my path.

"What are you doing here?" The man stands just a few feet from me. His t-shirt and jeans look wrinkled, like he slept in them, and he is only wearing socks. No wait. He's carrying boots, he just hasn't put them on yet. How'd he get up those stairs so quickly? And quietly? My eyes focus on the most gorgeous man I've ever seen. Poised like a police officer— feet shoulder width apart, hands on hips, boots hanging from one paw, stern furrowed brow, and hard glaring eyes. His deep, sultry voice makes my knees turn to Jello. In a sick and perverted way, I kind of hope he frisks me!

Chapter Two

Apprehension fills my core like a rain barrel during monsoon season. "I, uh, I… well." I straighten to my full height, which barely reaches his nose. While I am usually taller than my friends, this guy has a good five or six inches on me.

"Who are you?" I stutter and stammer, not sure if I should run back into the house and slam the door, or zip around this guy and run for my life down the stairs. Yeah, like that wouldn't kill me!

I choose neither and stand where I am, steeling myself and my attitude to mirror his. I cock my head to one side and slam my fists on to my hips, glaring at him for an answer.

His stern mouth, hidden behind a salt and pepper beard and mustache, morphs into a slight smile with a lifted eyebrow. Could he be any more gorgeous?

"I'm the guy" —he begins as he hops on one foot while sliding the boot onto the other— "who lives next door" —He switched to the other foot and slides the second boot on— "and keeps an eye on the place while my friend is out of town."

He sighs from the effort of balancing and hopping while putting on his boots.

I struggle to keep from giggling.

"Your friend, huh?" I fake bravado. "Well, he can't be too close of a friend if you don't realize he lost ownership of this house." I pause. It's none of this guy's business how the poor schmuck lost the house. There is no way I'm going to tell him I won the deed in a card game a couple of years ago. "Like, maybe two years ago."

I tilt my head and squint my eyes as if I am not afraid of him. Truth is, I think I peed a little when first I saw him. He looks like he could easily grab me and flip me over his shoulder to carry me like a fireman carries an unconscious person down the stairs and put me in my car. Of course, I know that wouldn't do me or him any good. Kiley is done for the day, maybe the week.

But he shows zero intimidation of me and doesn't move. "Really? You got proof of that?"

Golly, his smile does weird things to my insides. But I've gotta get a grip. Come on Maribeth, cowgirl up!

"Yep." I snap back, but I don't bother to mention the deed, the very proof that I am indeed the new owner, is in my car. I don't know for sure who this guy is. Just because he says he's a neighbor, I don't know that to be true. "You got proof you live next door?"

Now his smile is genuine. His stance relaxes a stitch. With a slight snort, he cocks his head back. "Yep."

Neither of us move. We are like two cowboys at high noon, standing in the middle of a dirt street, waiting for the other to twitch or draw their gun. The pressure is unnerving to me, so slowly, I open my fist and show him that I hold two keys.

His eyes swing down to my palm then bounce back up to my eyes. "You're holding keys that you took from the key box in the garage. That doesn't prove anything."

Why am I toying with this guy? I lift my chin. "How'd I get in the garage to get the keys if I'm not supposed to be here?" I punctuate my question by lifting my eyebrows.

His smile widens as if he is amused by me. "The code to get in the garage is pretty easy to figure out. I've told Frank he needed to change it to something less obvious than the year Hickok died."

I think back to the code. Everybody knows Bill Hickok died in Deadwood and that he was holding aces and eights when he was shot, but I didn't know *when* he died. 1876 didn't mean anything to me. There was no way I could have just walked up to the panel and guessed at that particular set of numbers.

"No. The numbers were given to me." I hesitate. "By, uh, Frank." Was that the guy's name? Seldom do I pay a lot of attention to who I play against. I recall a black man getting more and more agitated during the game and left forlorn. Was that Frank? I was there for the winnings, not to make life-long friends. He wrote those digits on the quit claim deed, obviously, so whoever won the house would have a way to get inside.

"Did he, now?" The guy squeezes his eyes to nearly closed, as if he were using his x-ray vision to see through me, searching for any lie indication.

My patience is wearing thin.

"Look, this is my house. Frank… uh, *transferred* it to me. That's all you need to know. Now, if you don't mind, I have things to bring in." I make like I am going to shove past him, but he doesn't move. I stop inches from him, looking up into his sea-green eyes. Heat radiates from his bare arms that bear intricate pictorial tattoos to his wrist. Without thinking I suck my lip into my mouth and bite down. God, he is so handsome!

"Uh, excuse me." I sound pathetically weak.

This guy's sheer presence was setting my hormones on fire. But he was being an ass. I could not let him get away with this pretense of protecting his neighbor's property. I knew the deed had passed into my possession over two years ago. So, ol' Franky-boy couldn't have been here for at least that long. Although the place had definitely been cleaned by someone. Was Frank still paying somebody to come clean the house on a regular schedule? I honestly had no idea.

I chance my assumption. "Do you do this to the cleaning crew when they come over? Or just out-of-towners, like me?" I say, hoping to get an answer to my question about the home's maintenance.

He shifted his weight. "No. I know Alice and her crew. I don't know you."

"Well, let me remedy that." I say with all the smart-assness I can muster. "I'm Maribeth. I own this house. Now, will you please get out of my way?"

He doesn't move.

This guy was really starting to piss me off. "Please." I say with very little cordiality.

He turns his head, now squinting at me from the corner of his eye. "Prove it."

"Oh! My! Goodness!" I bellow. "Let me go back to my car, and I'll show you the deed, my driver's license, my social security card, my NRA card, an ATM card, my AAA card, whatever you want, just so you'll leave me alone!" I didn't have an NRA card, My—but I was on a roll and just kept naming things that I could show him to prove who I am.

He jerks a nod and turns to trot down the stairs. I see a holster tucked into the back of his jeans. He didn't have time to put on his boots, but he grabbed his gun? Would he have shot me? I watch him for several steps and purse my lips tight to keep me from uttering the words twirling around my tongue.

"Is that a gun in your jeans, or are you happy to see me?"

STOP! I yell silently at myself! A grin curls on my lips. Man, he has a nice backside. Those jeans—

I shake my head. Stop it!

Then I start down after him in my non-acclimated pace. When I get to my car, he is waiting for me, breathing normal as you please. Me, I'm sucking air like there isn't any to be had on the planet. Just walking down the stairs made me winded all over again. Embarrassingly, I try to catch my breath by breathing through my nose, even though it sounds louder than if I just panted. I open my passenger door and reach in for the document I had carelessly left on the seat. Gosh, if I'd known there were people watching my every move, I would have locked the car.

Realizing I left the door to the house wide open, too, I suddenly fight the need to run back up and close the door. Like I could run those stairs! I roll my eyes at my own stupid idea.

"Here," I say, still trying to catch my breath, "is the Quit Claim Deed. Notarized and everything. I own the house. It's mine."

He looks the deed over as if he were the file clerk verifying it was legitimate, while I fish out my purse in case he wants to see my driver's license to prove who I am.

"I see." He says softly and hands it back to me. "So… My name is Jonathon Hemingway, but my friends call me Blaze."

I stare at him. *Blaze*? Is he kidding me?

"And what should *I* call you, Mr. Hemingway?" I know I'm being snarky, but for some reason I just cannot help myself.

He put out his hand to shake mine. I stare at his large hand. He has rough, callused skin but it looks like he uses hand lotion to keep it from being too rough. What does he do for a living?

"Blaze will be fine."

"Oh, so we are friends now?"

He grins again. "I'd like that."

That smile of his is full of ornery mischief and makes my heart pound and my legs feel like rubber. Or is it the altitude? Maybe I'm simply needing more oxygen.

I steel myself once more. "I'm Maribeth Thorp."

I put out my hand to grip his that has hovered this long. We shake as he continues, "Nice to meet you, Maribeth Thorp." He chuckles. "So, can I help?"

"What?" I jerk my hand back. I'm so confused. This altitude is befuddling my brain. Or his broad shoulders are doing it. I can see a shadow of a six pack under his t-shirt and want to run my fingers over it so bad! I'd trace each bulge and finish by circling my finger around his belly button—

What am I doing? I've gotta stop thinking like this! This guy nearly shot me for trespassing on my own property! I should be afraid of him! Or infuriated! Not lusting after his body!

"With carrying your things to the house. Do you need help?" He walked toward the back of my vehicle, waiting for me to open the door.

"I, uh. Sure." I squeeze my eyes closed. Why did I say sure? I don't want this brazen Nosey-Nelly helping me carry my stuff into the house. For one, I'm embarrassed how little I have with me. For two, I'm still angry that he accosted me at my own front door.

On the other hand, it isn't a bad thing to have someone so diligently looking out for the house. If my ex-boyfriend or anybody else decided to come uninvited, and I happen to not be home, I know *Blaze* would sabotage their attempt to surprise me.

I open the car door and start pulling out my clothes, in batches, on hangers. He opens the other side and pulls out a duffle and slings a black trash bag over his shoulder like a casual Santa Clause.

Lord have mercy, this guy is too gorgeous! I have got to get a grip before I embarrass myself even more.

"Okay, then," I say like we are old friends. "You go first. I'm not quite accustomed to this altitude yet, I'll only slow you down."

He nods and takes off trotting up the stairs. I watch before I join. Man, I like watching those jean pockets sway as he moves up the steps. By the time I get to the top, I'm gasping for air and leaning on the handrail. Just kill me now!

"Thank you." I breathe the words, because I cannot talk without heaving for air. He's leaning his back on the door frame with his arms crossed over his chest. I get a little sneak peek at that belly button I fantasized about earlier. It has just a hint of hair— I can't breathe!

He reaches out to take my load. Oh shoot! I was hoping for an opportunity to take this inside and collapse on the bed or couch or the floor, and rest a minute. Now all I can do is turn around and go back down for another load. I can't stand how incredibly handsome he looks!

"Look, I, I think… I got this… but… thanks for… for your help." I try to speak but I really do not have enough air in my lungs. I swallow hard. Blackness wavers at my peripheral. I fight to draw in air and let it out. Darkness closes in around me and I feel my knees buckle.

"I need t—."

Chapter Three

When I open my eyes, Blaze is sitting next to me on the couch inside my house. He's fanning my face with… something… the deed? I try to focus on what he's doing. Where'd he get that? Did I have it when I brought up that load of clothes?

"There she is." He says sweetly.

I pop up to a sitting position. "Oh my goodness, tell me I did not faint."

"Okay, you did not faint." He mocks me.

"UH!" I whine and cover my face with my hands while throwing myself back on the couch. "How embarrassing."

"Your tags are from Colorado, but… where did you come from?"

"Denver." I answer without even thinking about saying too much about myself to this man I don't really know.

"Hmm. The way you are reacting to the altitude, I thought you were from the coast or somewhere at zero feet from sea level." He smiles.

My heart leaps into a sprint for the finish line. "Stop doing that!"

"Doing what?" He cast his eyes over me, looking for something wrong.

"Stop smiling! I can't take it."

"Well," He chuckles. "What am I supposed to do, then?"

"I don't know. Go back to that stern cop-face you had when you first accosted me at the door."

"I didn't accost you, but I am a cop."

"What? You're a cop?"

"Well, I'm a detective, actually."

"Ah, that explains the gun."

He grins. "Well, this *is* Deadwood." He shrugs with that ornery smile. "And I didn't know who you were or what you were doing. A man has to be prepared when he confronts a potential burglar."

"How many burglars park their cars in the driveway and crawl up the stairs, with keys in their hands? Besides, you were in your socks. What were you planning to do? Throw your boots at me?" I giggle.

He just smiles.

I continue. "Seriously! Did I seem like a burglar to you?"

He shrugs. "I didn't know. That's why I ran over to check."

I stare at him. Man, those sea-green eyes remind me of the sunlight shining through a giant wave at the Emerald Coast of Florida. I could stare into these eyes all day long. I nodded. That was a reasonable answer. At least he didn't come over with his gun blazing…I suppress a giggle.

Guns a blazing! I shake my head. I cannot say that out loud!

"What?" He grins.

"Nothing."

"No, really, what?" He fixes his gaze on me. It feels… like I'm being hypnotized or something.

I cannot say this. I cannot— "I was just thinking… how lucky I am… that… you didn't come over here… with your…" I know I shouldn't.

But he insisted. Here goes nothing. "guns a blazing." My voice deteriorates into an uncontrollable laugh.

And then, I snort!

OH GOD! I snorted!

Now, he can't stop laughing.

I'm crying, I'm laughing so hard.

Then, suddenly, he stops! "Yeah, like I've never heard that before."

I force myself to stop laughing, wiping my eyes. He doesn't look amused… at all. Now I'm a little scared that I've upset him. "I-I'm sorry. You made me tell you. It's not my fault."

He nods with a half-twisted smirk on his mouth. "Yeah, I guess I did ask for it." He stands beside the couch. "Come on, let's get the rest of your stuff and put your car in the garage."

"Okay." I concede. "But, she'll have to be pushed."

He turns to see if I'm serious. I shrug and tilt my head. "She's deader than a door nail."

We walk together to those god-awful, lungs-ripping stairs. To be honest, I appreciate his help. I mean, since I insulted him, the least I can do is let him finish hauling my stuff into this house, like we really are friends or something, and then offer him a beverage of his choice. Assuming I have anything other than tap water.

"Many hands make lighter work, my Grandma Lizzie always said. The least number of trips I have to make the better. I certainly don't want to pass out again."

We walk down the stairs in a single file, and I grab another load of clothes on hangers while he grabs another trash bag and a tall laundry hamper. I open the trunk, and he grabs a suitcase from it. We make another trip to the house on the hill, slowly this time. I sit on a stool at the kitchen counter so I can catch my breath. He patiently waits.

"You want… something… to drink" I pant, not even knowing if I have anything. I open the fridge. It is full of bottled water. "Huh?" I turn to see if he sees this bounty of water. There's store-brand bottles, electrolyte infused water, and even fancy flavored and bubbly glass-bottled waters. "Wonder who stocks the fridge… and why?"

He shrugged. "Frank only came here once or twice a year, maybe he has Alice keep it stocked. Check the freezer."

My curiosity is jumping like a jackrabbit. I open the freezer drawer at the bottom and gasp. There are frozen steaks, chicken breasts, and packages of bacon and sausage. I turn to Blaze, my mind reeling. "When was the last time you saw Frank?"

Blaze looks at me, like he is considering if he should answer my question. "I'm not sure."

"Yeah, you are." I hold my gaze unwavering on him. He knows I know that he knows. "When?"

"Six months ago." I hear the hesitation in his voice.

"But…" I really don't understand this. "I've had this deed for over two years."

He shrugs. "What can I tell you?"

My mouth goes dry as dirt. "I'm confused." I cast my eyes around and find the deed. Blaze must have laid it on the coffee table. I lift it and read it over as if I don't already remember every detail.

"This is legit." I shake the quit claim deed. "I'm certain."

But who am I fooling? Even I can hear the uncertainty in my voice.

He nods and shrugs at the same time. "I believe you."

"Then… why is Frank still coming here?"

"I don't know. But I'll be happy to look into it for you, if you want." He says with all seriousness.

I can't believe he's willing to investigate this for me. "Surely there are more pressing matters in Deadwood than this." I give him a chance to back out.

With a tilt of his head and a lift of his brow, he says, "Not at the moment, there's not."

Chapter Four

"How are you going to 'look into it' exactly?" I curl my fingers into air quotes. "Do you like know-know the previous owner?" I sense myself cringing. I sound like a high school girl exposing my naïveté.

Blaze shrugs. Something I am noticing he does often. In a way it's endearing. On the other hand, I find it annoying. I really want answers. The thought of Frank Holmes showing up and just walking in is unnerving.

Should I get a gun? Or a guard dog? Change the locks? Set up security cameras or motion sensitive lights? I don't have the money for a good security system. I don't even have enough money to rescue a dog from the pound. I need to make my new home safe from the previous owner? Is Frank dangerous?

"I'll start with what I can find on his permanent address and go from there. I'm sure there's a trail to follow. He comes here infrequently. There has to be a purpose for coming here when he does. He seldom stays longer than a month, when he comes."

"Really?" My mouth flops open like a big-mouth bass. "So, he doesn't just come for a weekend retreat. He comes and stays for a whole month?"

"Yeah. He might show up on any given day, not just a weekend." Blaze recalls.

"Hmm." I ponder this information. "Why?"

"That's what I'll try to find out." Blaze assures me. He stands. "Come on, I think we can get the rest of your stuff with one more haul."

I begrudgingly slide from the stool and follow him down the stairs. I sure like the gorgeous view from here. The mountains are nice, too. He loads himself down with two suitcases and two lawn bags, I grab the last of the clothes on hangers, and the cappuccino machine.

Jason doesn't know I took it. I'm the only one between the two of us who ever uses it, so it's mine anyway. Although I expect to get a flaming text from him about it. I had agreed to only take my personal effects, like clothes and shampoo. But this machine, I consider my personal effect, too. And he can just get over it.

We trudge back up the long staircase and I, once again, collapse on the stool, panting for oxygen. He opens the fridge and takes out an electrolyte infused water, twists the top off, and hands it to me. "Here. Water helps."

"Thanks," I pant. I am from Denver. I don't get altitude sickness there. What's so different here in South Dakota? Maybe it really is Blaze's presence. Am I swooning because he so darn good looking?

"Well," Blaze cast his gaze over the pile of stuff we have dumped in the living room. "I guess my job is done here. I'll be going. Flash your porch light if you need anything."

"Seriously?" I smile. "Can't we just exchange cell phone numbers?"

"Sure." He pulls out his and I pat my pockets for mine. Where did I put my phone. "Ugh. I think it's still in my car.

"Tell me your number," he offers a solution other than me going down those stairs right now. "I'll call it and when you get around to retrieving it, you can save my number."

"Good idea." I hold up one exhausted finger in agreement. I tell him my number and he calls me, then hangs up.

"There. Done." He smiles. "Are you alright?"

"I will be." I assure him. "Go on, I'm fine."

He nods. "You really might want to think about changing the locks, considering."

"Yeah, I already thought about that." I am finally able to breathe normally. "Maybe tomorrow."

I know I need to make one more trip down those horrible stairs to get my phone and push my car into the garage. I might as well do it now. I say, "Hold up. I'll walk you down."

He shrugs. Cute.

We walk as we have several times now, with him in the lead and me focused on the w's on his back pockets. I go to my car, and he walks to the curb. I turn Kiley's key and listen to the whine and sputter of the engine. She's done all she can for one day. I try again, but she just won't turn over. A loud bang and a puff of black smoke is her final word on the matter. I take the key out and sigh.

I jerk when a tap on the passenger window startles me. It's Blaze. "You need a new car, too."

"No sheet, Sherlock." I'm being snarky again, but it just comes so naturally around this guy.

He smiles a half curl of his mouth. "I know a guy."

He pulls out his wallet and hands me a business card for a jeep dealer in Spearfish. There is a rubber ducky on the card and the tag line, "Come get ducked at Juneks Chrysler Jeep Dodge Ram."

"Cute." I state and hand him the card back. "Kiley's precious to me. She was my mother's. Besides, I can't afford a new car."

"You can't drive this one either. My friend will work with you. Mention my name, he'll get you a good deal."

I frown. "As long as I don't get 'ducked'." I quote the tag line. But I mean something much more vulgar.

"You won't, if you don't want to." He chuckles.

I look down at my lifeless dashboard. "How am I gonna get to Spearfish?" I whine to myself.

"I'm off tomorrow. I can take you." He offers.

"No." I jerk back. "You've done enough already."

He shrugs. "Well, how else can you get to Spearfish?"

"I don't know. Is there an Uber service here in Deadwood."

He snorted. "No."

"Well, what about Lyft?"

He shook his head in disgust.

"Taxi?"

"Yeah, but make sure you don't get Crazy Kate."

"Crazy Kate? That sounds… dangerous."

"I mean, if you want to take a chance with your life, go ahead, call a taxi, but I'm telling you, make sure you don't get Crazy Kate."

I sigh, defeated, again. "Okay. But not tomorrow. I need to get settled in first. I'll let you know when…" I lower my voice so Kiley can't hear me. "When I'm ready to go to Spearfish to buy a car."

His eyes tell me he suspects I've lost my mind. Maybe I'm crazier than this Kate who is not exactly a Taxi driver. "Okay. Let me know when."

I stand next to Kiley's driver's seat. One hand on the steering wheel, the other on the door frame. "A little help?"

He tips his head back and positions himself at her rear bumper. I lean in over her driver's seat and slip my phone into my back pocket, then stand, ready. We push her into the garage. He gives me a two-finger salute and walks away. I get out of my poor, dead car and lock the doors. At least the key fob still works. Closing the garage door as I leave to climb those stairs one last time. A hot bath and bed should be the only things on my mind, but Blaze and his nice fitting Jeans fills my thoughts instead, that and recovering from the climb.

Chapter Five

Despite Blaze's warning, I google for a taxi service in Deadwood and downloaded the app on my phone. I fill in my current location, and request a driver to come as soon as possible. Almost immediately my phone chimes with a text message.

A photo of a thin-as-a-rake woman with light gray hair, in fact she appears to be bald at first glance and the label, Katlin Kroger, pops up underneath her headshot on my screen. Could Katlin be Crazy Kate that Blaze warned me about. I switch back to the app page, looking for a customer service contact link to request another driver, but I get another text message and clicked over on it.

"Your driver will arrive in eight minutes," the text reads.

Hmm, surely it's not Crazy Kate. Her name is Katlyn. I peruse the headshot. She doesn't look so crazy to me. A latent hippie, maybe, from the 60s, definitely. But not crazy.

I stand on my tippy toes and angle my head just right, so I can see from the laundry room window the street and my driveway. It's not the most comfortable way to watch for my ride, but I know from experience that if I'm not ready to leap out my door the minute Crazy Kate, er, I mean Katlin, pulls into my driveway, Blaze will probably pounce on her.

Would he be so bold as to tell her to go on? Would he insist on giving me a ride himself? Anger roils in my gut, as I diligently watch for the first sign my ride has arrived. Obviously, he has a lot of nerve from the way he crept up on me yesterday. He just might run the driver off, since he specifically told me *not* to call for a taxi. Like what I do is any of his business.

Sure, he offered to give me a ride, but where I need to go, I don't want him to be privy to. It might have been kind of him, but I don't feel all that comfortable having a police detective aware of my business. Besides, I don't really know this guy.

Riding around town with a total stranger is foolish, even if he is my over-the-top handsome neighbor. I understand that Ted Bundy was pretty cute in his own right.

Of course, I'm perfectly comfortable riding with an absolute stranger who just might be Crazy Kate as my Taxi driver. Yeah, I recognize the irony. It's the anonymity that makes the Taxi driver a better choice. Since they are bonded professionals, they are also sworn to secrecy, right? Like a doctor. What happens on a Taxi ride stays on a Taxi ride. And it's nobody's business where I am going this morning. Assuming I can find what I need.

I do not want *Detective Blaze* to know anything about how badly I need money, a lot of money to replace my savings taken from me by the settlement with Jason. Blaze doesn't need to know how I go about getting it. For all he knows, or needs to know, I had the money in my account all along.

But this amount is not something I can walk into any one of the casinos here in Deadwood and win. This kind of cash that I need in order to start over here in Deadwood, can only be won in an underground, high-stakes game.

I glance out the window at the garage where Momma's car is in her final state of rest. Poor Kiley, she's all I have for a buy-in. With the car as my collateral, I'll strategically start at a lesser table with a two-thousand buy in and work my way up to the bigger winning game. I'll probably be out all night.

I hesitantly pull her title from my "important papers" binder and slip it into my backpack purse, just in case, to prove I can afford to get in on a game. Too bad I'm not near where Uncle Donald could help me get into a game, like he did when we lost Daddy. It's not like I'm putting up my only house for collateral, like dad did, and I promised I'd never do.

I won't mention the car's not running at the moment. Once I win, assuming my luck holds out, I'll move up to the bigger game, and walk out with what I need.

Should this be *the time* that Lady Luck isn't my friend, I'll lose my precious car. I sigh heavily. And… have to deal with the fact that she's not running when they come to claim her. A shiver of reality rakes my spine. I could seriously be in big trouble.

I close my eyes and steel myself. This is my only option for getting back on my feet. I'll deal with what happens afterward if I have to.

Bones heal. Was that what Daddy said before he played the game where he lost everything?

I focus on my driveway. I go through this every time I decide to attend a game to save my butt. Moving to Deadwood has not changed that for me.

"This'll be the last time, I promise." I tell my momma as if she were standing there with me.

I get a text, accompanied with the head shot again, stating, "Your Taxi driver has arrived."

I grab my little backpack purse and rush out the door, locking it behind me. Hurrying down the stairs so I can beat Nosey Nellie to the Taxi. I get there before Blaze can ruin everything. I've never been to Deadwood in my life, but surely with this town's history and reputation, it won't be hard to find exactly what I am looking for and I know how to find it.

The woman from the photo is sitting sideways in an older model, moss green, Chevy Blazer. There is no identification on her vehicle to indicate she is a Taxi. That's odd. Her boney elbow is propped across the back of her seat so she can see me climbing into her vehicle.

"Are you Katlyn Kroger?" I ask.

"Yep." She nods a quick nod.

Her salt-and-pepper hair is buzzed really short on her head. That was what made her look bald in the headshot. Her super-short bangs look as though they were recently dyed with a purple color. Her headshot had been taken prior to the coloring. Like her photo, she is very thin, but not hollow-eyed like she's starving to death. Maybe a vegetarian, who never eats fat or red meat. I want to offer her a steak dinner, but really, it's none of my business. She reminds me of the Woodstock hippies that Grandma Lizzie spoke about often when she reminisced about "the good ol' days."

"Hi." I pant breathlessly from my little race down the stairs. "I'm Maribeth. Thank you for coming so quick."

"Yeah," She glances down the street. "My name's Kate." She shuffled with some placards in her seat. "Listen, did you call for an Uber or a Taxi?"

"I, uh, I called for a Taxi." I answer wondering if I heard her right.

She nodded quickly and stuck a yellow and black "Taxi" sign by a suction cup, after she licked the inside of the plastic cup, in her front window beneath her rearview window.

"Where you need to go, Hun?" She smacks on gum.

I smile at her. Should I get out of her vehicle immediately? Awkward silence sat between us. "I, uh…"

She waits patiently for me to answer, but her eyes keep darting toward the street. When I requested the ride, I didn't include my exact destination. Instead, I put, "will discuss with driver." So the app would let me submit my request. I am positive she's not who I send the information to. I have no idea how she intercepted the request, but she's here, and something about her makes me want to stay in the blazer and see how this all turns out.

"I'm not sure. Let's just head toward downtown and I'll figure it out as we go."

"You want to see where Bill Hickok died, or take a tour of one of the brothels?" She asks, not turning around to drive like I had hoped.

"No. I'm not looking for a tour, but I'll know it when I see it."

She shrugs. "Sure, but I gotta know what your destination is, Hun. That's how I know what to charge you."

"Okay." I roll my eyes. "Then I want to go from here to the other end of the downtown area, then double back up the other side. What will that cost me?"

She puts something into her phone and turns to look at me. "That would be this much." She holds up the phone screen to face me. It's looks like a paypal account page, to me.

"Okay." I say and pull out the cash.

She takes her time, entering my payment into her phone, tucking the bills into her t-shirt. Was she wearing a bra? Most latent hippies I know don't. She adjusts her cleavage as if the money made her uncomfortable and mutters something about a sports brassiere. Ah that answered my question.

"Could we get going?" I say impatiently, glancing toward Blaze's property.

She turns around with her skinny long arm draped over the back seat and looks right at me. "Now, there's one thing I gotta tell ya." She smacks her gun. "If I should happen to get pulled over. You are not a paying customer. We are pals and you asked me to give you a ride. Okay?"

I grin from ear to ear. Yep, this is indeed Crazy Kate. This is going to be a really interesting experience. "Sure."

She pulls out of my driveway and heads toward Main Street. I crane my neck to see if Blaze is watching us leave as we pull away. His house looks dark. I wonder if he's watching with his lights off so I can't see him. I feel so defiant as we pull away.

But I'm not being defiant! I remind myself. Then flop around and sit back in the seat, buckling my seat belt. I barely know the guy. Why do I feel so beholden to him? I'm a grown woman and can do whatever I want, thank you very much. We turn north on Main Street where half the touristy businesses are located. The speed limit is such that I can easily peruse each storefront on both sides of the street.

I'll know what I'm looking for when I see it. It won't necessarily look seedy. My gut will tell me when I find the place where I can get the information I need.

Finally, I see just the place.

"Here." I announce. "Pull over."

She does, but then quickly yanks the placard out of the window and buries it under some McDonald's wrappers in her front seat. "Remember, you didn't pay me." She blurts.

"Wha—?" I start to say as a police officer walks up to Kate's bronco. "Miss Kate," he says in a sing-song manner. "You're not giving rides to paying customers, again, are you?"

He looks at me in the back seat.

"No." She shakes her head. "This is my friend…" She turns and speaks out of the corner of her mouth. "What's you name again?"

"Maribeth." I whisper.

"My friend, Maribeth. She's new to town and not sure where nothing is, so I suggested I take her in grand style, like I was her chauffeur, all fancy like that." She laughs in a hysterical, crazy sort of way.

The cop glares at me. "Is that right?"

I nod. "Kate's been a real life saver, Officer."

I want to get out of the bronco, but I don't dare since we are busted. The cop smiles at Kate. "Okay, just make sure you don't, Kate. You know we've got our eyes on you."

She nods like a child agreeing, but with her fingers crossed behind her back.

There's something going on here. I don't know exactly what. But if I didn't know better, I'd say the police of Deadwood know perfectly well what Kate is up to but they ignore it and basically let her get away with it. Interesting.

Finally, she turns in her seat to put her elbow over the backrest to address me. "You want me to wait?" She said as if nothing had just happened. She eyes the storefront quizzically. "You've paid for a lot more miles than this." She whispers like the cop might hear her even though he is three storefronts down the sidewalk by now.

"No. I'll call for another Taxi when I'm ready to leave."

She laughs. "Oh, no, that won't work. Here." She shuffled through some things in her passenger seat and handed me a business card with nothing but a phone number. "Just text me directly when you're ready. That way we can settle your account based on how much farther you go with me."

She has a motherly look of concern written all over her skin-and-bones face.

I smile to reassure her that I'm fine. "Okay. I'll" —I wiggle my phone— "text you when I need you again."

She nods. "Okay, Hun. I look forward to giving you a lift again." She grins while glancing toward the street. "You seem like good people." She says with a genuine smile.

I stand corrected. She *is* crazy, but not the scary crazy like Norman Bates's mother in Psycho. More like fun-to-tell-my-friends-about-later kind of crazy. I like this woman. I return her smile. "Thanks, Kate."

She hesitantly pulls away. I turn and walk into the Deadwood Tobacco Company. To my right is a sales counter, with a wall of accessories for cigar smoking: Humidors of all sizes, cutters and punches, fancy lighters, simple lighters, ashtrays of every size, material, and design, ventilating smoke eater machines, posters, and other sundry items imaginable that would be associated with smoking cigars. To my left is a huge, walk-in humidor where all the cigars are displayed for sale. As I walk further into the store, I see what I'm looking for. A lounge.

Where there's a lounge, there are waitstaff who know stuff.

I slide onto a bar stool with my back to the stage, where apparently, by the looks of the abandoned drum set and mic stands, they have live bands. I see a screen at one end of the stage. Maybe even karaoke? A thrill runs down my spine. I love to sing, and Karaoke is one of my tamer vices. It's the only way I can pretend to be a real singer and belt out the tunes I love the most.

I make a mental note to ask as I peruse the large glass front humidor displaying several different brands and types of cigars. At the other end of the polished bar are mirrored glass shelves with rope lights underneath, filled with every bottle of alcohol known to mankind. Standing behind the bar is a man who watches me with an amused look on his face.

He either thinks I'm lost and don't know what I'm doing or he's that good of a server and is letting me look over the choices before he approaches me. "What can I get you, Miss?"

I smile. "A cream soda, and…" I peruse the cigars as if I don't remember what I just saw. He doesn't know I have eidetic imagery. "I'll have an Oliva, Melania Maduro."

"Good choice." He remarks and unlocks the glass cabinet with a key on a roll-back lanyard at his waist, handing me a cellophane-wrapped cigar. He turns his back to me and walks to the liquor end and brings back a crystal glass and a dark brown bottle of cream soda.

"Mmm." I smell the cigar through the wrapper, then unwrap it. I pull a cutter from my purse and snip the end, then pull out a torch lighter and warm up the end of my cigar before puffing on it. After a few puffs to get it well lit, I pour my cream soda and take a sip. Savoring the two flavors, I close my eyes. "Mmmm."

The man is smiling at me when I open my eyes again. "You new around here?" he asks.

"I am." I smile and take another puff-sip combination and enjoy the two blending in my mouth.

"My name's Maribeth Thorp." I put out my hand and shake his. Taking a chance my next statement will grant me the leverage I need, I say, "As in Eddie Thorp's daughter."

I watch for his reaction.

He does not disappoint. His brow lifts and his eyes widen. "I see."

He busies himself polishing the spotless bar, but I know I have his full attention.

"I was hoping to get some information."

"Yeah?" The man wipes the bar with a white rag. "What kind of information?"

"You obviously know who my father was, what kind of information do you think I'd be looking for?" I say coyly.

He glances at me. "Why you asking me?"

I smile, tilting my head with a slight shrug of my shoulder. "Something tells me that anybody who runs a cigar lounge in an age of anti-tobacco restrictions, even in a town like Deadwood, would know a thing or two, that's all."

"You want to gamble? Go over to the Cadillac Jack's Gaming Resort." He apprehensively wipes the already clean bar top.

"Yeah, I'm looking for something where a gal can set herself up pretty good afterward, you know?"

His eyes flicker to me and back to his polishing cloth. "I see. Well, I don't know nothing about nothing like that. Sorry." He puts away his cloth and walks to the other end, where he lifts a section of the bar, and exits the server area. I sip my cream soda and puff my cigar patiently. I know how this works, and I know I'm in the right place to get what I want.

As I near the end of my cigar and my cream soda, a large, rotund, dark-haired man comes from the back. He scans the empty lounge, as if there were people to look over, then walks to me. "You asking about karaoke night?"

I pause. Ah, he's speaking in code. "Yeah."

He jerks a nod and shifts a toothpick in his mouth to the other side. "A pretty young thing like yourself ought not go looking for trouble."

"I'm not. I promise." I smile.

"You might wanna come back tonight when we got an open mic for karaoke." He points a thumb over his shoulder at the empty stage. "Ya think you could sing something by Patsy Cline?"

I grin ear to ear. "I love Patsy Cline!"

"Yeah, I thought maybe you might." He tilts his head and slides his brows up in an uncaring sort of gesture. "We got extra parking in the alley. The street's too crowded most of the time. I reckon we'll see you there?"

"Yes." I reply.

"Okay. Just be careful. I wouldn't want a pretty young thing such as yourself to get in over her head."

"Oh, I won't, I assure you."

He still looks concerned for my well-being.

I stare at him. "I've sung on a karaoke stage many times. I'm pretty good, if I do say so myself." I say as I lock my gaze with his. "I'm not scared."

"You should be." He states.

"Should I?" I ask.

A white business size card appears in his large hand and with one meaty finger he slides it over to me. I lift it and see two words. Green Door.

He turns and saunters to where he had emerged from the back. I put the card in my purse and put my cigar in the glass ashtray so it can go out on its own. I walk to the front of the shop, lifting my phone. I thumb over to the Taxi app and request my friend to come pick me up.

Quietly, I sing to myself, "I go out walkin', after midnight…"

Chapter Six

Crazy Kate drops me off at my house just before daybreak. I was shocked when I texted her at six AM and she replied. When she dropped me off at the mouth of the alley, so she wouldn't know exactly where I was going, it was midnight. I really figured she wouldn't be available six short hours later. But I sure was glad when she replied, and I found her parked in the same spot she had dropped me off by the time I had counted and stuffed my money in my backpack. I didn't want to linger in that alley any longer than I had to.

The green door, it turned out, was not an easy thing to find, nor was it very green. More like a dull, rusted olive colored cellar door. So low to the ground, I had to stomp on it, rather than knock, in order to gain access. I have to admit, at that point I was nervous. A very large, dark faced man opens the door and peeks out at me. I say, "Patsy Cline."

He smiles and hurries me inside. My heart slowly stops racing as I settle into the familiarity of it all.

I sit in on a game as common to me as washing my hair. It goes on for hours. In the end, I win, receiving a large pot of money, a Rolex watch, my car's title, and a silver rodeo buckle. My winnings are gathered for me while I text Kate to come get me. I put the bundle in my backpack and step out into the alley. Dusk is gently lighting the sky above my head. Kate's Bronco turns down the alley.

"Oh, Kate. Thank you for getting here so fast." I say as I slid into her backseat.

"Not a problem. I don't sleep much anyway." She waved my gratitude away with a slender, bony hand. Her nails had a fresh coat of Purple Passion nail polish. Just since Midnight, she had painted them. She really didn't sleep much at night.

"Besides, I still owe you for how you over paid me earlier today, er, I mean, yesterday. But after this, we're even." She turned to glare at me, like I would challenge her on the issue.

I nodded with a smile. "Can we get going?"

"What chu afraid of? Did chu do something illegal while I was gone?" Her eyes twinkled with mischief.

I shrug. "No, not really."

I'm not afraid of being accused of a crime. You see, while the host who organizes a high stakes card game is the one who is civilly and/or criminally responsible should any lawmen show up, I, as a player, am not breaking any laws, and the money I win is not illegal. My greatest fear is getting robbed before I can get home. I hug my backpack to my chest. If only she knew what I'm carrying inside this pack. She might be the one I fear robbing me.

"Listen." Kate looked in her rearview mirror and put the bronco into drive. "You don't ever need to be afeared of anybody when you're with me." She grinned in her mirror, making reflective eye contact with me. "I got a concealed license to carry, and I always carry. You're safe with ol' Kate."

"Good." I choke out the word. Knowing Crazy Kate is carrying a gun doesn't exactly put my mind at ease. On the other hand, if anyone did try to steal my backpack, and Kate was truly willing to protect me, her passenger, I would be safer than if I attempted to walk home alone. I tried my best to let that sink in and melt the tension in my back muscles.

Pulling into my driveway, the tension that remained in my shoulders begins to release. "Thank you, Kate." I say and get out.

"Sure thing, Hun. I'll just wait here, 'til your safe inside." She smiles and waves goodbye like we are old friends. I don't mind Crazy Kate being my friend. I like eccentric people, so long as they aren't dangerous.

I jerk a nod and head for those stairs. My regular-size backpack, which I now carry instead of the little one that serves as my purse, isn't heavy at all. Surprisingly, a hundred thousand dollars in one-hundred dollar bill-bundles only weighs a little over two pounds. It's the stairs to my house that nearly kill me when I climb them as stars fade and dawn takes over. Kate idles in my driveway until I flicker my porch light, hoping Blaze does not mistake it for a signal that I need him for some weird reason. I am safely inside my house. Kate can leave. And she does, with a quick flick of her high beams.

"Geesh! Please don't wake Blaze." I mutter.

The money I won is clean and I can use it to buy whatever I want as soon as I want to. I can pawn the buckle and trade the watch for a lady's Rolex at a jewelry store, but that's not my concern right now. I probably should replace Kiley.

My heart aches. I love that car. It's all I possess that was my Momma's. I know it's ridiculous but I would rather spend the money to have her fixed, no matter the cost, than to replace her. Her deceased carcass still sits in the garage. Surely I can find a mechanic who's willing to revive her one last time.

I'll deposit the money and have my account transferred from Denver to Deadwood's Wells Fargo Bank. Anything more than ten-thousand dollars will be reported to the IRS, but that's okay. I don't mind paying my fair share of taxes.

I start the coffee machine while I gasp for oxygen. Will I ever get acclimated to Deadwood or these stairs to my house? And I need a nap. Then I'll go to the bank. Once they update their system with my new address and make my deposit, I won't need to do anything other than order new checks. My daytime Taxi driver and friend, Crazy Kate, can drive me to the bank. Maybe Kate will know of a reliable mechanic's shop where I can, hopefully, get Kiley running again.

That's the plan.

I'm still panting from the walk up the stairs and let the backpack fall to the floor as I stagger to the bedroom and fall face first on the mattress. I'm not as young as I used to be. Staying awake and alert all night is hard on this thirty-one-year-old body. I sigh, pull the bedspread to fold it over me like a taco, and fall asleep.

At some point, the front door slams open!

I sit straight up in bed!

It's bright daylight. Why would anybody break into my house in daylight?

Someone is banging into the wall as if they stumbled, and walking like an elephant across the entry, into the living room. They certainly are not trying to be quiet!

I hear two loud thumps. The person must have dropped something. Dead bodies? Luggage?

My eyes are wide, but my mind is in a fog. Am I dreaming? I don't wake well. I slide out from under the cover, thankful I fell asleep fully clothed, and tiptoe to the door of my bedroom.

I freeze, casting my eyes about for a weapon. There's nothing but the lamp on the nightstand. I lift it, yanking the cord out of the socket, which whips around and hits me smack in the face! I'm not quiet either.

I *do* need to buy a gun. A shotgun, so I can cock the shell into the chamber letting that be the first thing a burglar hears before I confront them.

"Who's there!" I bellow in as deep of a voice as I can muster. The last thing I want is to sound like a scared girl.

"What?" A man replies. "Who's in my house?"

My house? I sigh. Pretty certain I know who is out there. "Frank?"

"Yeah." He sounds less aggressive.

"Crap!" I whisper. I knew this would happen. I just didn't think it would be so soon. Where was Blaze's super curious neighborhood watch when I needed it?

"Who are you?" He calls out.

I walk out to where he can see me. "I'm Maribeth Thorp." In my all black, head to toe, I probably look like a cat burglar to him. The expression on his face tells me he's alarmed at the sight of me. I continue to explain. "The person who won this house from you in Vegas two years ago.

Why are you still coming here? You don't own this house anymore."

He hangs his head. "Well!" The two poorly packed cases fall over at his side. "My wife don't cotton to my gambling, especially when I lose, and she kicks me out of our house when I come home broke. So, I come here 'til she cools down. I've been coming here for years. Even though I lost the deed. You have never showed up, so I reckoned you didn't really want the house and it was safe for me to continue to come here to wait Milly's temper out."

He looks up. Sadness permeating his watery eyes. "I reckon you had changed your mind."

"Yeah, I changed my mind." Is all I can say. He's pathetic. "Didn't you notice my Kia in the garage?

"Well, yeah." He scratched his stubbled chin. "I just figured someone parked it there."

"Someone did park it there, Frank. Me! The owner of the house!" My temper is starting to escalate.

"I know." He moves to the kitchen and takes out a Pellegrino water.

I stare at him. The audacity! He doesn't even recognize that he's trespassing on my property! "Frank!" I shout. "You don't live here anymore!"

Just then the front door flies open and Blaze rushes in. His sea-green eyes are dark, like when the sea is engulfed in a storm. "Frank!"

"Whaaat?" Frank's dark eyes bulge with aggravation. He sighs, as if he is getting tired of hearing his name. Slowly, he turns around to see my neighbor standing at the door.

Blaze darts his eyes to me in the hall. His gaze drops to my black leather boots and back up, ending at my leather jacket. "Where you been?"

"Really? Now?" I sputter. "Both of you, get out of my house!"

Frank jerks as if I had doubled up my fist and reared back to hit him. Blaze takes Frank by the shoulders and steers him toward the front door. "Come on, Frank. Come over to my house, I'll explain what's going on."

I run up and kick one of Franks bags. I yell, "And get your stuff!"

Blaze has an ornery grin on his smart-aleck face, but Frank looks terrified of me. The fear in his face breaks my heart. Flashbacks of the men who kicked me and Momma out of our house after Daddy lost everything, smolder in my mind. It was the worst feeling ever. Even though Frank lost ownership to this house two years ago, he obviously had not accepted that it was no longer his. I could understand that since I had taken this long to show up and claim it. Did he have somewhere else to go? Besides Blaze's house? Where was he living when he wasn't here?

"Hey, wait." I step up behind them.

Blaze and Frank each hold one of Frank's suitcases with tips of clothing poking out like it had been haphazardly filled and slammed closed. "What's your story, Frank?"

Frank sighs heavily. "My wife don't like me gambling, especially when I lose." Frank's eyes darted to the ground. Shame filled his dark face. "Especially, then. And she kicks me out. I usually come here, until she cools down and will let me come back. This is essentially my dog house."

I tilt my head, considering what he is telling me. "Well, it's a mighty nice dog house."

"Yeah, I retain a cleaning service so it'll always be ready for me." He looks up. "After I lost it, I chanced coming here after one of Milly's fits, and prayed you hadn't showed up. Which you hadn't and didn't, for a long time. So I just kept coming back, when I needed to."

I nod. "I see." I say empathetically. "Look, Frank. I need the house now. Is there nowhere else for you to go… when Milly is mad at you?"

"Sure. Of course." He said, but my instincts knew he was lying.

Blaze put his arm around Frank, like a big brother. "Frank, you can come stay with me. I got a spare bedroom."

"Really?" I say, feeling like I just beat a puppy.

Blaze glances at me with a frown as if he just witnessed me beating said puppy. "Yeah, sure."

They shuffle out my door. I rush up behind them. How could I do that to someone after what I've been through? I lean my back on the door and slide down to crouch against the door. Burying my face in my hands, the tears start against my will. "I'm such a bitch!" I sigh.

I hate getting woken from a good sleep!

Chapter Seven

I like using a person's first name when I am the customer. If I am made aware of their name, I use it as if we are old friends. I feel like it makes them feel seen. Why else would a person wear a name tag, or tell you their name, if they didn't want you to use it when you interact with them?

I wave at Kate in her illegitimate taxi after I walk to the front doors of the Wells Fargo Bank with my regular-sized backpack slung over my shoulder, so she knows she can leave. With a wave, she drives away. Approaching the first available teller, I smile and place my backpack on her counter. Inside are neatly packaged one-hundred-dollar bills which are my winnings from last night.

"Hi, Michelle." I say like I've known her for years, but in truth, I read her name on the cheap plastic sign by her window. "How's it going?"

She smiles a practiced response. "Hi. How can I help you?"

I'm prepared to explain how I came by the money. "Can you believe it? A long-lost uncle left me this backpack full of *money*. I feel like I'm living out a mystery novel!" I laugh. "Suddenly, I got all this cash. It makes me nervous, though! I want to get it deposited as soon as possible."

Michelle's eyes grow wider and wider as I speak. You'd think this much money would be old hat to her, but apparently not.

"So I was wondering, if I give you my account number from Denver, could you transfer it to here and let me put this money in the account here in Deadwood?"

"Wow." Michelle eyes the backpack. "Sure. Let's start by counting it." She takes the backpack across her counter and turns, hesitates, then turns back to me. "Would you like to go with me to the counting machine?"

"Sure." I say, knowing she figures I don't want to let the cash out of my sight. Little does she know,

I watched Big Mike, the guy from the cigar lounge, count and package it as he put it in there last night. I follow her through the dutch door and into a back closet-like room where she takes off the bindings and runs each bundle through a machine that counts the bills lickety-split.

"That never gets old." She almost giggles.

"Yeah." I nod.

"So what do you do for a living." Michelle makes small talk while the machine whirls and pops.

"I'm a professional organizer." I state proudly. After all, I *am* proud of what I do for people.

"What does that mean?" She turns from the machine to give me a questioning brow.

"I take chaos out of people's lives and leave them refreshed and organized."

"Like that gal on TV? Uh, Marie Kondo?" She re-bundles each set of one-hundred-dollar bills while we talk.

"Yes. Exactly like that."

"Really?" She squeals. "And you live here in Deadwood?"

"I do."

She looks around, as if we are conspiring about something naughty, then leans into me. "If I got some of my girlfriends together, would you meet, say for lunch, and, I don't know, set up some time when you can help each of us declutter?"

I'm stunned and thrilled at the same time. "Sure."

What do you know? I might have clients! "When did you have in mind?"

Stacking the bundles, she put them in a cloth money bag and returns to her teller counter, which I appreciate. The less anyone standing around in the bank knows about how much money I just brought in, the better as far as I'm concerned. "I'll finish this transaction for you and give them a call."

"Cool." I say nonchalantly, but inside, I'm jumping up and down. I just might have clients here in Deadwood already!

"Would you like an account balance?" She asks routinely.

"No," I reply. "I'm pretty sure what I've got."

We giggle.

"Okay, give me just a sec." She lifts the bank phone to her right, and dials a number, obviously making the personal call look like a business call. I smile at her ingenuity.

"Hi, Cindy, it's Michelle." There's a long silence. "Yeah, I was wondering if you and the girls could get together for lunch tomorrow?" Another long silence. This girl must be long winded when she answered. "Yeah, I have someone I'd like you to meet." She glances at me with a smile. "No, it's not a guy!" She giggles. "Actually, she's a woman living here in Deadwood, and she is a professional organizer, you know, like that oriental chick on tv who declutters—"

"Right." Michelle smiles at me again. "Yeah, her name is, She looked back at her computer screen, "Maribeth Thorp."

"Yes, I know, we all need to hire her, for sure. Okay, tomorrow at 11:30, say—" She looked at me like I have an answer. I shrug.

"Buffalo Bodega…" She looks to me for confirmation. I don't know any of the restaurants yet, so I just nod approval.

"Yeah, and I'll bring her with me, so y'all just meet us there… Right. 11:30." Again she looks to me for approval. I nod, not sure if she means she's planning to pick me up or have me meet her there.

Did she see me getting dropped off by Kate? I frown.

Her eyes sweep the bank, as if she just realized she's on a personal call during business hours and quickly concludes with, "Okay, I gotta go." Then hangs up.

"All set. Do you know where the Buffalo Bodega is?"

"Not sure, but I've got a friend who can drop me off." I tell her.

"Great. Let's get there about ten minutes earlier than Cindy and them, so there's no awkward uncertainty when you walk in."

"Sounds good. I'll bring my portfolio, too." I am smiling like the Cheshire Cat. I couldn't be happier. "Thank you."

"Oh, no." She shakes her head. "Thank you! I'm so glad you came to my window."

"Me, too." I say and slide my empty backpack onto my shoulders. "See you tomorrow."

"Yes. Oh, hey!" She says like an afterthought. "They have karaoke on Saturday nights, do you sing?"

I smile. "As a matter of fact, I love Karaoke."

"Great, let's plan to go back tomorrow night."

"Excellent!" I give her a thumbs up and leave the bank. Lifting my cell phone, I text Kate to come get me if she's available. She is. I'm not surprised.

Kiley's replacement would have to wait another day. Mentally, I make a task-note to tell Blaze I would not need him to take me to Spearfish tomorrow. Maybe not the next day, either.

Sadness shoves my joy for having potential clients out of my heart and weighs down heavily like a huge sumo-wrestler flopping down for a rest. How could I just trade Kiley off? I would rather find a mechanic who was willing to do what it took to fix the Kia and keep her running, at least one more year.

Although Blaze has insisted I go with him to Spearfish and talk to his friend about a trade, I will, to ask him if he knows a guy or gal who could work on Kiley, instead. If he doesn't, I'll ask around until I find the right person for the job. Maybe Big Mike knows someone?

Once again, I don't have to do what Blaze thinks is best. I know what is best for me. After eight years of being with a man who held me accountable to him for everything he said I should do, I am free and will make my own decisions. It felt good to have that freedom. I refuse to allow myself to slip back into a domineering relationship with anyone every again. Especially where Kiley was concerned.

And now, I have money in the bank to do what I want. I have friends that I feel good about, and tomorrow I meet with potential clients. Things are looking up. Moving to Deadwood is paying off. I pat my backpack where I had tossed the account receipt. In more ways than one.

I'm building a new life here in Deadwood with all my favorite things, Karaoke, Cards, and Clutter.

THE END

Love the story?

Write a review. Thank you.

Next book is Hidden Aces in Deadwood

About the Author

Lynn Donovan is an author, playwright, and director who spends her days chasing after her muses trying to get them to behave long enough to write their stories. The results are numerous novels, multi-author series, anthologies, dramatizations, and short stories.

Lynn enjoys reading and writing all kinds of fiction, historical western romanceparanormal, speculative, contemporary romance, and time travel. But you never know what her muses will come up with for a story, so you could see a novel under any given genre. All that can be said is keep your eyes open, because these muses are not sitting still for long!

Oops, there they go again…

Want more?

You can learn more about Lynn when you follow her on her Facebook Author Page at https://www.facebook.com/LynnDonovanAuthor, join her reading group on FB at Books by Author Lynn Donovan @ https://www.facebook.com/groups/BooksbyAuthorLynnDonovan/, her website LynnDonovanAuthor.com and Twitter @MLynnDonovan,

For more publications by Lynn Donovan go to: Amazon.com/author/ldonovan

Appreciation

Thank you to everybody in my life who has contributed in one way or another to the writing of this book. My husband, my children, my children-in-law, and my grandchildren. You all are my unconditional fans. My BETA reader and grammar guru who make me look gooder than I am. [Bad grammar intended.] My fellow author friends who chat with me daily to exchange ideas, encourage, maintain sanity, and keep me from being a total recluse/hermit.

Mostly I thank God for the talent he has given me. I hope to hear you say, "Well done, my good and faithful servant," when I cross the Jordan and run into your arms—Many, many years from now. :).

Newsletter and a Free Gift for You

Hey! Thank you for purchasing and reading this book. I'd like to give you a parting gift to show my appreciation. Sign up for my newsletter at lynndonovanauthor.com/newsletter. I will send you an e-copy of a collection of short stories I wrote purely for your entertainment. I will happily send you this e-copy for FREE, if you ask. I will also add you to my NEWSLETTER list and you will receive up-to-date information on new release before anyone else.

This book will **not** be sold anywhere, at any time, I am keeping it exclusively for you, my readers, and only if you ask for it.

Thank you again, and God Bless.

~Lynn Donovan